名流詩叢 22

永久酪農場 Perpetual Dairy

妳悄悄愛上我
然則妳為何
突然？

我是卑微詩人
沒有顏色的照片
無生命。

阿米紐‧拉赫曼 (Aminur Rahman) ◎ 著

李魁賢 ◎ 譯

自序

　　什麼是詩？柯爾律治說：「詩是最精練的字，安排在最佳秩序。」梵樂希說：「詩的第一行來自天上，其餘必須你來寫。」華茲華斯說：「冷靜中回想的感情。」麥克萊希說：「詩應該不是意義，而是存在。」濟慈說：「詩應該像樹長出葉子。不然，寧願什麼都沒有。」

　　實際上，詩到底是什麼？世界各地的詩人，為什麼在寫詩？為什麼愛詩人到處都有？台北是繼承詩永恆力量的都市。為什麼對這種美眾說紛紜的人，強烈愛好詩？我們真的知道什麼是詩嗎？為什麼我們愛詩？詩人為何寫詩不停，並無明確定義，也沒有任何解釋，為什麼詩愛好者繼續吸取內在感覺的芬芳。

　　每個人都有詩心，有些人賦予名稱加以表現，

另方面，有些人具備養成的技巧，這些是真正的詩愛好者。即使如此，全世界愛詩人數仍少。為什麼？天性、文化、素養、傳統，在在促動人的柔性角落，使其狂熱酷愛詩。

現實裡沒有獨特的詩語言或色彩，詩人在世界的一個角落寫詩，鼓舞並渴望在世界另外角落的愛詩人。意思是我們都是人類，或許膚色、天性、行為、語言有所差異，但我們是同樣心靈所創造。因此之故，為什麼少女會愛上世界不同地方的情人，因此之故，為什麼人會為來自異方的人犧牲生命，同樣緣故，來自世界一端的詩人寫作，會與另一端的愛詩人互動。詩的力量超乎一切，而觸動內心歸一。詩的力量創造人性。詩的力量幫助人活出新生命。

現代孟加拉詩始自詩人麥可・默圖蘇丹・杜塔，他出生於孟加拉，但孟加拉詩的主流來自諾貝爾桂冠詩人泰戈爾。他創作大量詩世界和創作，諸如短篇故事、小說、散文、藝術和無數歌曲。印度西孟加拉省和孟加拉的人民，仍然在鋪設遵循其作品的創作道

路。另一位孟加拉文學上的偉大詩人是卡濟‧納茲魯‧伊斯蘭，他也在寫詩、散文、小說、短篇故事和無數歌曲領域，留下創作珍寶。繼其後，在上世紀三十年代出現五位大詩人，吉班納蘭達‧達斯、舒得興達拉納茲‧杜塔、佛陀德維‧博斯、維斯努‧德維、阿米雅‧恰喀拉瓦諦。每一位都創造建立了各自不同風格和文學世界。他們所作的主要貢獻是透過翻譯，把外國文學，特別是歐洲文學，帶進我國文學裡。這五位當中，吉班納蘭達‧達斯開啟描寫自然的現代詩新門扉。吉班納蘭達‧達斯是繼泰戈爾之後，最重要的孟加拉詩人之一，也不可否認是孟加拉語先進現代詩人之一，當然一直是最偉大的孟加拉詩人之一。然而，他在西孟加拉省和孟加拉國以外，卻鮮為人知。

五十年代的孟加拉詩人把西方孕育的現代性要素，引進到孟加拉境內的孟加拉語詩。佛陀德維‧博斯以孟加拉語精彩描述法國詩人波德萊爾詩，引導五十年代的孟加拉詩人進入到現代歐洲詩的版圖。他

們也受到德語詩人里爾克、英語詩人葉慈和艾略特作品深刻影響，在他們本身的原創性和個人特性之間，並無扞格。

七十年代中期，為實現我國家生命，在解放戰爭中喪失三百萬條人命，民主價值被棄於地，屈服在暴虐獨裁下。所以，在民主制度瓦解後十年內，正是專制徒然試圖在孟加拉土壤裡挖根的十年。這段時期裡，犯罪、腐敗、社會不公、政治不平等、經濟不均，在官方縱容種種不義實務下，在我們社會萌芽，把非民主規則永植入國內。在此期間注入我國詩壇的青年血液，起義對抗非民主、不受歡迎的政治體制，加以控訴。雖然少數人寧願避開政治酷熱和灰塵，仍然隱身在愛情和浪漫的夢土。

孟加拉語詩在孟加拉，還是比在印度西孟加拉省更繁榮。蓋因1952年成為第一種語言，且已具有語言歷史。孟加拉國民已經為孟加拉母語犧牲生命。每年2月21日慶祝語言節，成為孟加拉最熱烈的慶典活動。新孟加拉詩兼容傳統和現代主義向前進，雖然有許多

經歷已體驗到後現代主義。

　　最後，我想提到的是，我們亞洲人對西方文學和詩，已有充分理解，我們有些人深具博識，因為語言之故。我堅信是時候了，應該嚴肅探究亞洲詩和文學翻譯成今日廣用的各種語言。我們知道亞洲詩從泰戈爾迄今，只有一位諾貝爾獎得主，且因為是靠他個人的努力。所以，如果我們希望我們的詩，在世界上受到肯定和欣賞，那麼我們必須採取個人策略和組合論壇。我曾經把台灣著名詩人李魁賢的詩譯成孟加拉語。這才剛起步，他也同盡心力。讓我們攜手合作，把亞洲詩傳布到全世界去。

　　　　　　　　　　　　　阿米紐・拉赫曼

　　　　　　　　　　　　　2016年5月12日

Preface

What is Poetry? Coleridge says 'Poetry is the best word in best order.' Paul Valerie says, 'The first line of a poem comes from heaven, you have to write the rest.' Wordsworth says, 'Emotion recollected in tranquility.' Archibald MacLeish says 'A poem should not mean but be.' Keats says 'A poem should come as a leaf to a tree. If it does not, it is better it does not come at all.'

Actually what really is Poetry? The poets all around the world, why are they writing the poetry? Why the poetry lovers all around? Taipei, the city that has inherited eternal strength of poetry. Why the people of this discrete beauty have the intense love for the poetry? Do we really know what is poetry? Why do we love poetry? There is no real definition of why poets keep on writing poetry neither there is any explanation of why the poetry lovers keep on absorbing the aroma of its inner sense.

Every human has poetic soul some gives it a name by expressing it, on the other hand, some have this knack of culturing it and those are the real poetry lovers. Even than the number of poetry lovers all over the world is small. Why? The nature, the culture, the practice, the heritage which expedite the soft corner of people and makes them crazy to adore poetry.

There is no distinct language or colour of poetry in reality, poets from one corner of the world write poetry and that inspires and aspires the lovers in the other corner of the world. This means we are all human beings, may be colour, nature, behavior, language are different but we are created from the same soul. That is the reason, why a maiden loves the man from different part of the world, that is the reason, why men sacrifice life for men from different end and for the same reason, when poets writes from one end of the world and the same is reciprocated by the poet lovers at the other end. Poetry is that strength which rises above all and touches the inner being of one. Poetry is that strength which creates humanity. Poetry is that strength which helps human to live a new.

The modern Bangla poetry began from poet Michael Madhusudan Dutta who was born in Bangladesh, but the main stream of Bangla poetry comes from Nobel laureate Bengali poet Rabindranath Tagore. He has created enormous world of poetry and creativity such as stories, novels, prose, art and memorable songs. The people of West Bengal of India and Bangladesh are still paving the paths of creativity in line with his works. Another great poet of Bangla literature was Kazi Nazrul Islam, who also has left behind a treasure of creativity in the field of writing poetry, prose, novel, short stories and memorable songs. After them five great poets have evolved in

永久 酪農場

the thirties. These poets have been Jibanananda Das, Shudhindranath Dutta, Buddhadev Bose, Vishnu Dey and Amiya Chakkravarty. Each of them created and established their own different style and literary world. The main contribution they made was to bring foreign literature into the country by translating, particularly European literature. Among the five Jibanananda Das opened a new door of modern poetry depicting nature. Jibananada Das is one of the most important Bengali poet after Rabindranath Togore, without a doubt one of the leading modern poets of Bengal, and certainly one of the greatest Bengali poets of all times. Nevertheless, he is a poet who is hardly known outside West Bengal and Bangladesh.

Poet of the fifties of Bangladesh introduced elements of modernity as conceived in the west in Bangla poetry in Bangladesh. It is through the masterly rendering of the French poet Baudelair's poetry in Bangla by Buddhadev Bose that Bangladeshi poets of fifties have been ushered into the realm of modern European poetry. They are also profoundly influenced by works of German poet Rilke, English poet W. B. Yeats and T. S. Eliot, without compromising their own originality and individual characteristics.

In mid seventies democratic values, for the realization of which in our national life three million lives were lost in the liberation war, were dashed to the ground and gave way to despotism and dictatorship. The decade following the downfall of democracy was, therefore, a decade of autocracy trying in vain to strike roots in the soil of Bangladesh. This is the period when crimes, corruption, social injustice, political inequalities and economic inequities started germinating in our society under official patronized all kinds of unfair practices to perpetuate their undemocratic rule in the country. The young blood infused in the world of poetry of this country during this period revolted against undemocratic, unpopular political

永久 酪農場

dispensation and denounced it. Although few were preferred to stay away from the heat and dust of politics and remain closeted in the dreamland of their love and romance.

Bangla poetry is more nourished in Bangladesh than in West Bengal of India. This is because the first language being and having the history of language during 1952. Bangladeshi people had sacrificed lives for their mother tongue Bangla. Celebration of 21st February as language day is one of the most vibrant and celebrated occasion in Bangladesh. New Bangla poetry is moving forward along with its tradition and modernism although a lot experience has been experienced with the post modernism.

Last of all I want to mention that we Asian have a good understanding and some of us have in depth knowledge of western literature and poetry and that is because of language. I strongly believe that it's about time that we take serious look into translations of Asian poetry and literature into various languages widely spoken these days. We all know there was only one Nobel Prize winner for poetry from Asia 'Rabindranath Tagore' till date and was because of his personal effort. Therefore, if we want our poetry to get recognized and appreciated in the world then we have to take focus measures personally and in the combined forum. I had translated poems of great Taiwanese poet Dr. Lee Kuei-shien into Bangla. It is just a beginning and Dr. Lee is doing the same. Let's join us and spread our Asian poetry all over the world.

Aminur Rahman

12 May 2016

永久 酪農場

目次

自序 003

    Preface　008

愛情 1　019

    Love : 1　020

愛情 2　021

    Love : 2　022

愛情 3　023

    Love : 3　024

愛情 4　025

    Love : 4　026

愛情 5　027

    Love : 5　028

愛情6　029
　　Love：6　030

愛情7　031
　　Love：7　032

生命1　033
　　Life：1　034

生命2　035
　　Life：2　036

雕刻　037
　　The Sculpture　039

啊啊　041
　　Hai Hai　042

殺我吧　043
　　Kill Me　044

孤苦依賴　045
　　Solitary Dependence　049

混亂　053
　　Confusion　056

心岸 059

    Heart's Shore 061

為妳 063

    For You 066

妳 069

    You 072

盈月夜 075

    Full Moon Night 078

灰姑娘 081

    Cindrella 084

想念妳 087

    Missing You 089

月亮 091

    Moon 094

我心靈 097

    My Soul 101

永久酪農場 105

    Perpetual Dairy 107

寶貝　109
　　Poppy　111

等妳千年　113
　　Waiting for You for Thousand Years　117

自殺　121
　　Suicide　122

自願流亡　123
　　Self-willed Exile　126

簡便包裝的生命　129
　　A Life Wrapped in Ease　136

鄉愁　143
　　Nostalgia　145

愛情 1

困難重重
凡事似乎漫無目標
只是
浪費時間。

不需理解
不需付出
我心堅定
然而，一切明白。

Love : 1

A lot of difficulty

everything seems aimless

Just

a waste of time.

Without understanding

without giving

my heart is stiff

even though, all is clear.

永久 酪農場

愛情 2

閉著眼睛

我在選擇鑽石

我心快慰

雖然萬失無所獲

Love : 2

With eyes closed

I make a diamond-choice

My heart is blissful

Though everything is lost

愛情 3

妳悄悄愛上我

然則妳為何

　　突然？

我是卑微詩人

沒有顏色的照片

　　無生命。

Love : 3

You love me quietly,

why then the abruptness

in you?

I am a lowly poet,

a picture without colour

lifeless.

愛情 4

靠

惡夢　　這

一人　　日子

能　　　藉

活得　　記憶

合理　　無法

　　　　持久

Love : 4

with

nightmares   the

one   days

can   pass

live   memories

reasonably.   fail to

last

永久 酪農場

愛情 5

我內心天空容納妳，藍妮*

銀河外的星星

河上蓮花

嶄露新女性。

*Nilima在梵語中指「藍色」，也是女性名字。

Love : 5

My heart's sky contains you, Nilima

A star beyond the galaxy

A lotus in the river

Emerging as a new woman.

愛情 6

愛情飛走了

飛、飛到觸碰妳

觸碰到妳後，回到

　　　我唇

但仍然似乎

有的給有的沒給。

愛情仍然留在

妳心裡。

Love : 6

Love flies away

flies, flies to touch you

After touching you, returns

    to my lips

But still it seems

some of it is given and some not.

Love still remains

in your heart.

永久 酪農場

愛情 7

長久以來，我一直在找妳
從在此巷到彼弄
　　結果，始終無消息。

在群眾躲雨處
在鳥孵暖的巢內
若找到妳，我自己的鑽石
就回到我村莊
和我所愛的人成家。
我會盡心工作
生活無後顧之憂。
只要留下妳，我的愛

Love : 7

For so long, I've been searching for you

in this alley and that lane

    The result, always negative.

In a crowd seeking shelter from heavy rains

In a nest where a bird heats her hatchings

If I find you, my own piece of diamond

I shall return to my village

set up home with my beloved.

I shall work my heart out, and

there will remain no folds in my life.

Only you shall remain, my love

永久 酪農場

生命*1*

繼續　無窮盡

無形骸的藍天。

子宮內生命

克服一切阻礙的河流。

不良的謠言

印度大麻熔汁

人是殺人機器

造成時疫，結束。

Life : 1

Continuous   endless

Structure less blue sky.

Womb's life

an all-conquering river.

Undesired rumours

Melt-fluid *ganja*

Humans are killer-machines

that lead to epidemic, the end.

生命2

不久前，我

絲毫沒有感覺——

到底我在哪裡，

我不記得。

生命中一瞬間

吹一口氣

就隨風而逝。

我能吃、能走，還能

與女人做愛？

不，不，我毫無記憶。

我什麼事都不記得，

甚至連

我自己的往事。

Life : 2

Just a while back, I

was very far away from my own senses --

where exactly I was,

I do not remember.

A few moments from my life

merged with the wind with a mere blow

from my mouth.

Was I eating, walking, or was I

making love to a woman?

No, no, I remember nothing.

I cannot remember anything,

not even

my own lost time.

永久 酪農場

雕刻

從濃霧海角
我雕刻妳的體型——
精雕細琢、整個上午。

我閉眼，坐在
濃霧漫漶間
當霜降
在我頰、耳鼻上。
同樣的手，
同樣的唇、同樣眼睛——
我如此容易看清——
妳的胴體浮在河上；
我要抵制它流動。

妳的形體開花，自我解放，
留下陽光
和霧無常的身體。
妳與我的心靈糾葛──
其根基、底座和深度。

The Sculpture

From the mist's dense cape

I carve your body's shape --

gently sculpting, all morning.

With my eyes shut, I sit

amid the fog's heavy sheets

as its frost settles

on my cheek, ear, and nose.

The same hands,

the same lips, the same eyes --

I find them with such ease --

Your torso floats on that river;

I shall conquer its flow.

Your figure blossoms, freeing itself,

leaving behind sun's light

and fog's ephemeral body.

You're entwined with my soul --

its root, plinth, and depth.

啊啊

鞋
頭　　　灰
書　　　無
甘塔*　　碗。　　　我在
鱸魚　　歌　　　哪裡？　啊啊
妳。　　穿衣　　妳？　　啊啊
床　　　妳　　　妳　　　啊啊
對。　　注意　　吃，　　啊啊
壕溝　　保持　　吃　　　啊啊
水。　　臼杵　　到心滿　啊啊
萬事　　像書，　意足，　啊啊
順利。　破　　　日——　啊啊
　　　　傘。　　長，　　啊啊
　　　　　　　粉白——　啊啊
　　　　　　　月亮。　　啊啊

*甘塔（Kantha）是孟加拉手繡輕毯。

Hai Hai

shoe

head   ash

book   no   where

kantha   bowl.   am I?   hai hai

rui-fish   song   you?   hai hai

you.   dress   you   hai hai

bed   you   eat,   hai hai

right.   watch   eat   hai hai

ditch   keep   to heart's   hai hai

water.   mortar-pestle   fullness,   hai hai

everything   like book,   day-   hai hai

agreed.   torn   long,   hai hai

                umbrella.   starch-   hai hai

                                moon.   hai hai

永久 酪農場

殺我吧

以妳專情的心殺我吧。

藉妳的性行為粉碎我。

用瘋人的瘋狂謀殺我。

在妳內心裡焚燒我。

以妳的創造力殺我吧。

藉性的濕泡綿殲滅我。

用妳的性感帶摧毀我。

以妳的愛撕裂我。

咬我咬我胯部。

在我欲仙欲死時抱緊我。

Kill Me

Kill me with your dedicated heart.

Reduce me to smithereens through your act of sex.

Murder me with madman's madness.

Burn me in your heart.

Kill me through your creativity.

Annihilate me with the wet-foam of sex.

Destroy me with your erogenous zones.

Tear me apart with your love.

Bite me bite my crotch.

Embrace me in my death's ecstasy.

孤苦依賴

這些日子，我很少不開心，
只針對永生悲傷。

我孤苦依賴在半夜甦醒，
感到腳底發冷；
我張大眼睛，看到無窮遼闊
包圍存在的庭院空間，
正像妳的影子。

妳是誰？妳是誰？

有時妳感到熟悉，
有時，又不熟。

有時妳內心光明自在，

有時，又充滿懷疑。

有時妳看似在此世間，

有時，又在他界。

有時妳像小孩，

有時，又無盡沉默。

妳是誰？妳是誰？

夜顫動，心旌搖搖

好像樹葉對微風訴情意。

水波在無瀾河面上動蕩，
魚靜止不動，
星星在編織夢想。

妳是誰？妳是誰？

沉浸於無聲世界，
我獨坐
等晚紅流失。

另一夜晚來臨，
動，動身，轉身低語
自殺的衝動。

妳是誰？妳是誰？

這些日子，我很少不開心，
只針對永生悲傷。

Solitary Dependence

Very little, can hurt me these days,
my grief's address lives on forever.

My solitary dependence awakens at midnight,
I feel the cold under my feet;
my eyes, wide open, sees the endless expanse
encompassing a courtyard-space of existence,
just your shadow.

Who are you? Who *are* you?

Sometimes you feel familiar,
at other times, unfamiliar.

Sometimes the play-of-light lives in you,

other times, only pre-dawn's darkness.

Sometimes you seem so simple,

at other times, full of doubt.

Sometimes you seem to be in this world,

other times, in some other.

Sometimes you are child-like,

at other times, just endlessly silent.

Who are you? Who *are* you?

The night trembles, the heart flutters

like leaves whispering to the breeze.

The waves stir on the placid river,

the fish are motionless,

and the stars weave dreams.

Who are you? Who *are* you?

Engulfed in a soundless world,

I sit alone

as the ruddy-night bleeds away.

Another night arrives,

moves, moves on, turns back to whisper

its suicidal urges.

Who are you? Who *are* you?

Very little, can hurt me these days,

my grief's address lives on forever.

混亂

一點一滴，萬物崩潰了——
磚、石，連我的心也崩潰了。

即使曾經塗過石灰
也未鬆散——紅、藍、綠、黃——
我們無論拿到什麼色，都混在一起。
並非都能混拌，但我們不斷嘗試。

我要保持呼吸躺在河川胸膛，
活著仰望天藍，
聞花香保持活力充沛。

然而，混亂發生了。

石灰剝落——

磚、石，還有我的心。

這是我散步、聊天、生活的

方式，有時候甚至死去。

無人知道此事，無人明白。

河川明白嗎，或是天空？

天空會明白嗎？

花卉會明白嗎？

他們真正能明白一切嗎？
或者只是在混亂中安慰自己？

生命和生命領悟——什麼關係？
活潑和停滯——什麼關係？
人類和猴猿——什麼關係？
喜歡和愛戀——什麼關係？

一點一滴，萬物崩潰了——
磚、石，連我的心也崩潰了。

Confusion

Little by little, everything is crumbling --

bricks, stones, my heart too is crumbling.

Even though there has been

no slack in applying enough plaster -- red, blue, green,

yellow -- whatever colour we get, we mix.

They do not always mix, yet we keep trying.

I want to keep breathing and lie on the river's breast,

live by seeing the sky's blue,

keep alive by smelling the flower's scent.

Nevertheless, the confusion carries on.

The plaster peels off --

bricks, stones, and my heart.

This is the way I walk, talk,

live, and sometimes even die.

Nobody knows that, nobody understands.

Does the river understand, or the sky?

Does the sky understand?

Does the flower understand?

Do they really understand everything?

Or just console themselves in confusion?

Life and life's realisation -- what's the relation?

Living and stagnation -- what's the relation?

Human beings and monkeys -- what's the relation?

Liking and loving -- what's the relation?

Little by little, everything is crumbling --

bricks, stones, my heart too is crumbling.

心岸

妳不在那裡，
我怎麼辦？
愛情的
粉筆記號。

要死，
要活──
都是
同樣事。

何時我
和妳

去
心岸？

漂走，
畫夜——
和妳在一起。

葉落，
花開——
在心岸。

Heart's Shore

You aren't there,

what shall I do?

Love's

chalk-marks.

To Death,

To Life --

it is all

the same thing.

When will I

and you

go to

the heart's shore?

Float away,

day and night --

with you.

Leaves shed,

flowers bloom --

on heart's shore.

永久 酪農場

為妳

如果妳真的要，
沒有什麼事
我不能為妳辦？

我可死，
我可殺，
或者
我可傷心，
永遠走在
無止境的小徑。

如果妳真的要，
沒有什麼事
我不能為妳辦？

我可刮掉

鬍髭，

而

甚至放棄

抽

大麻。

如果妳真的要，

沒有什麼事

我不能為妳辦？

立起，

坐下，

或
在午陽下，
追
妳。

如果妳真的要，
沒有什麼事
我不能為妳辦？

For You

If you really want,

there is nothing

I can't do for you?

I can die,

I can kill,

or I

can be saddened,

and walk

the endless paths forever.

If you really want,

there is nothing

I can't do for you?

I can shave off my

beard and moustache,

and

even give up

smoking

ganja.

If you really want,

there is nothing

I can't do for you?

Stand up,

sit down,

or

in mid-day sun,

chase

you.

If you really want,

there is nothing

I can't do for you?

永久 酪農場

妳

妳今天是完全不同的人樣
在深深冥想中獲得一些訊息
來自現實的訊息，不安再現

妳始終是櫃台服務員，跟著思想
熱情、主動、堅持、宣告、全景動作
但摻雜感情和出人頭地的經驗歷練

妳可以盡情夢想美的旋律和浪漫的月光
盡一切所能拚命延展無邊無際無窮盡的美
到處繞行使河流整日整夜潺潺音響

妳突然改變自己創造出一個邊界

進行預先設想規劃好的計畫

深思熟慮，身無分文

亦即

獨

特

無

與

倫

比

的

妳

但在下方

夢正在哭泣

繼續不停止地

請勿逕直通過，這些都是寶！

YOU

You are a completely different person today

With deep meditation you got some messages

Messages from reality, restless and recurrence

Always you are a frontbencher, move with thought

Passion, proactive, persistent, proclaims, panoramic

But blended with emotion and emerged experience

You can make your dream with a melody and moonlight

Extend it as much as possible with the beauty of boundless

It moves around making a river jingle all day all night

Suddenly you have changed yourself to create a border

and proceed with a pre-conceived plan

profound, poundless

that is

u

n

i

q

u

e

y

o

u

but down below

dreams are crying

continuously endlessly

please don't pass through, these are precious!

盈月夜

我帶來沙漠的愛

我帶來海洋的愛

我帶來山脈的愛

我也帶來我的愛！

我要貼哪一個地址！

月、夢、無盡時間，何處！

妳屬於哪個地址！

東、西、南、北，何處！

太重帶不動

加上音樂更重

加上回憶更重

加上欲望更重

我要貼哪一個地址！

我曾向廣大綠地詢問妳的地址！

我曾向白雪詢問妳的地址！

我曾向瀑布詢問妳的地址！

無人知道妳的地址！

我把全部愛保留在天空

以閃爍的群星圍繞

就在月亮旁邊！

盈月夜妳在此可找到這些！

當妳聽到河流的音樂

當妳聞到玫瑰的香味

當妳感到臉上的微風

盈月夜妳可以擁有這些！

Full Moon Night

I have carried love from the desert

I have carried love from the sea

I have carried love from the mountain

I have carried my love too!

Which address will I post!

Moon, dream, endless time, where!

Which addresses you belong to!

North, south, east, west, where!

It is too heavy to carry

It is heavier now with music

It is heavier now with memories

永久 酪農場

It is heavier now with desire

Which address will I post!

I have asked your address from enormous green!

I have asked your address from white snow!

I have asked your address from the waterfall!

Nobody knows your address!

I have kept all loves in the sky

Surrounded by glittering stars

Just next to the moon!

In a full moon night you can find them there!

When you can hear the music of the river

When you can get the smell of roses

When you can feel the breeze on your face

In a full moon night you can take them!

灰姑娘

妳半夜裡在我面前出現！
當我關閉夢境所有門扉
當我可聽到黑暗聲音
突然妳在我面前出現
就像灰姑娘走出童話故事
我已經足足等待千年
提著我空空的夢籃子等待。

當我問空氣「妳在哪裡？」
當我問夜晚「妳在哪裡？」
當我問月亮「妳在哪裡？」

全部都說「我不知道！」

突然，空氣對我耳語

「對，她正走過來啦！」

妳就從童話故事出現我面前

妳問我「為什麼在半夜醒來？」

我告訴妳「我想要尋夢」

我也對妳說「我要開啟夢境門扉」

妳同我廝守幾分鐘

共享音樂「愛情讓我們活下去」

妳突然消失不見蹤影

從空氣、以太、到處失蹤！

我一再嘗試要找到妳

可是妳無形、無法捉摸又不可交融

我到處找不到妳

妳無情消失為了救我

卻時時刻刻殺我千遍

流血夜硬撐過，心喃喃不已。

Cindrella

You have appeared to me at midnight!

When I have closed all my dream doors

When I can hear the sound of darkness

Suddenly you have appeared to me

Appeared out of fairly tales just like Cinderella

Thousand years I have been waiting for

Waiting with my empty basket of a dream.

When I have asked the air, 'where you are?'

When I have asked the night 'where you are?'

When I have asked the moon 'where you are?'

Every one said 'I don't know'

Suddenly the air whispered in my ear

'Yes, she is coming!'

And you have appeared to me from fairly tales

You questioned to me 'why you are awake at midnight?'

I told you 'I was trying to find a dream'

I also told you 'I would like to open my dreams doors'

A few minutes you were with me

Until we enjoyed the music 'love can make us alive'

Suddenly you vanished

Vanished from air, ether and from everywhere!

I was trying and trying to find you

But you were invisible, incredible but immiscible

I could not find you anywhere

You have disappeared ruthlessly to save me

But every moment killed me a thousand times

Bleeding night passed on with heart murmur.

想念妳

想念妳日日夜夜

想念妳在我工作場所

想念妳在我沉思中

想念妳在我旅行照相時

想念妳在我快樂時

想念妳當我對月傾訴

想念妳在我悲傷時

想念妳當我聆賞音樂

想念妳在我長途駕車時

想念妳在我健身房內

想念妳在我擔任志工時

想念妳在我所有美好報價中

想念妳在我孤單時

想念妳在我呼吸空間裡

輪到我還是妳——

我們兩人彼此想念！

Missing You

Missing you all day and night

Missing you at my work place

Missing you at my meditation

Missing you in my journey and pictures

Missing you in my happiness

Missing you while talking to moon

Missing you in my sorrows

Missing you while listening music

Missing you in my long drive

Missing you in my gymnasium

Missing you in my voluntary work

Missing you in all lovely quotes

Missing you in my loneliness

Missing you in my breathing space

It's my turn or yours-

both of us missing each other!

月亮

幾乎每天妳對月亮談心

有時盈月有時缺

是妳孤單時的伴侶

月亮熱情佇望聆聽妳

無論妳旅行何處，總相隨

保加利亞、希臘，甚至德國

好像妳的寵物

聽妳指示，無論妳要做何事

總是隨候妳差遣

順從妳命令

陪妳吃，

跟妳說話

甚至睡覺。

在妳苦惱的日子裡始終陪妳

給妳精神支持。

妳哭時，他也哭

不讓妳知道

妳笑時，最高興

妳與月亮共享夢境

協助妳建構，更為成熟

我長時間追隨妳的月亮

對妳的月亮感到嫉妒

在我談話時干擾我

在我夢中干擾我

在我與妳交友時干擾我

我真的會發瘋不知道

如何處理妳的月亮…

Moon

Almost every day you have been talking to your moon

Some times with full moon or fractioned

It is the main companion in your loneliness

The Moon stands watch and listens to you passionately

Whenever you traveled, you carried it with you

Bulgaria, Greece or even in Germany

It seems a pet of you

It listens to your instructions, whatever you want to do

It is there with you

It obeys you

Eats with you,

Talks with you

Even sleeps.

In your distressed days it was always with you

Had given you mental support.

When you cried, it cried too

Without letting you know

When you laugh, it is the happiest

You have been sharing your dream with the moon

It helped you to construct, even to maturity

I am following your moon for a long time

I am feeling jealous of your moon

It is disturbing me in my talk

It is disturbing me in my dream

It is disturbing me to make you my friend

I am really mad and don't know

How to handle your moon…

永久 酪農場

我心靈

我沒有什麼話好送給妳

唯有我的感情呈現

如何對妳說明

這是我心靈，我的存在！

我知道妳正在等我

難道不能接受我感情，我心靈

同妳一起，同妳的孤單

若妳觸碰我心靈就會感受

這些既溫柔又巧妙

耐心等待與妳相會！

午夜

大家都已入睡

無數星星大肆閃爍

我心靈在強風中顫抖

直透成簇小豆蔻

多麼不同氛圍

多麼勁暴隱喻

內心與變形混同

在孤獨中奇異掙扎！

我心靈，我的存在四處活動

在天然找尋──同樣石頭

同樣鳥、同樣樹葉

妳安置你心靈連同詩魂所在

既無退化又未復發

觸及看不清楚的美！

心靈與寧靜之間無間隙！

以枯葉或變色葉

肯定或勝利，無論妳顯示什麼跡象

紅或黑，無論妳穿什麼衣服

我心靈靜靜坐妳身旁

沒有話說看著妳一哩又一哩

海又有海，世界又有世界

不言不語，可憐到腐朽！

語言在此無用——

唯有我的感情呈現急於觸及妳！

答案是激動、異樣瘋狂！

My Soul

I don't have any words to send you

only my feeling is present

How can I explain to you

this is my soul, my existence!

I know you are waiting for me

can't you take my feeling, my soul

with you, with your loneliness

if you would touch my soul then will feel

these are soft and delicate

waiting to meet you with patience!

At the midnight

when everyone has gone to sleep

when numerous stars are blinking enormously

my soul is shivering in the strong wind

biting in clustered cardamom

What a different atmosphere

what a mutinous metaphor

mind mingles with metamorphosis

strange struggling in solitude!

My Soul, my existence moves around

searching in nature - the same stones

the same birds, the same leaves

Where you have put your soul with the muse

neither the rust nor the recurrence

touches the beauty of blindness!

No gap exists in the soul and serenity!

With the dry leaves or with coloured ones

Yes or victory, whatever sign you are showing

red or black whatever dress you are wearing

My soul is next to you sitting motionless

without words seeing you mile after mile

Sea after sea, world after world

Speechless, piteous in moldiness!

Where words are useless-

only feeling is present to touch you eagerly!

Impassionate, exotic madness will be the answer!

永久酪農場

　我的永久酪農場每天伴妳開工
　結束時，妳還在那裡。

　在白天與達格瑪故事之間
　在咖啡與袖扣故事之間
　在世俗觀與性慾增效故事之間

　當妳正坐在我前面
　以炯炯眼神注試著我
　我撫摸妳的臉頰
　握妳的頭髮，吻妳久久
　兩個舌頭在波動
　抱緊妳從頭頂到底

抱得緊緊直到半透明油燈熄滅

夾妳、撞妳、咬妳

我強硬展現在不平的山谷

隨著激烈不完美顫動飄飄然

妳忙著醃漬美食

我動身大膽進入危地

搜尋熱情重力

搜尋未寫的詩篇

搜尋夢幻火龍果

我的永久酩農場每天伴妳開工！

Perpetual Dairy

My perpetual diary's everyday starts with you

And at the end, you are there.

In between stories of days and Dagmar

In between stories of coffee and cuff links

In between stories of secularism and sexual synergy

When you were sitting in front of me

Looking at me with sparkling eyes

I have touched your check

Held your hair, kissed you for a long time

Both tongues would move with the waves

Grasped you from top to bottom

Held you tightly till the translucent torch went out

Bit you, smashed you and ate you

My strong presence in the uneven valley

Flying with enormous faulty fluttering

You were busy with pickle pamper

I have moved myself with daring into danger

Searching the gravity force with passion

Searching the poetry that was unwritten

Searching the dream dragon root

My perpetual dairy's everyday starts with you!

寶貝

我的朋友呀！我的親親呀！

妳突然害怕了

一點點不安，一點點不自在

這就是生活，亂七八糟的生活

但妳堅強又親切

把苦悶寄託在骰子

妳知道，妳是誰！

女性、鹿、謹慎、小心——

看看前面，有什麼東西

在等，別忘記分享

確信妳會成功

第十感積極，足夠療傷止痛

還有誰能比得上妳

在排隊裡妳會看到許多污穢

妳無可比擬、很棒

嚴格、守時、精明、不隨便

會送妳到不同高度

像風箏伴月飛……

我始終在那裡注意妳快樂

我的朋友呀！我的寶貝呀！

Poppy

O my friend! O my dear!

Suddenly you are in fear

A bit of uncertainty, a bit of restlessness

This is the life, a life of a mess

But you are strong and nice

Put the agony in a dice

You know, who you are!

Fair, deer, mere, do care -

See in front, something is there

Waiting, don't forget to share

You will be a winner for sure

Tenth sense is active, enough for a cure

Who can be better than you

A lot of dirt you may see in a cue

You are incomparable you are good

Strict, punctual, smart and of a non casual mood

Will send you to a different height

Fly with the moon as a kite......

I am always there to see you happy

O my friend! O my poppy!

等妳千年

我急著等候妳
我試著從早到晚找妳
左右中間到處
花裡、石裡，或揮發大氣中
到處找！

妳在哪裡！
妳是水中的美人魚？
妳是花園裡的仙女？
妳是兼屬於風和水？

為何我不是鱷梨三明治！
為何我不是人間毛毯！
為何我不是熱茶！

當妳整夜在煮東西

我可聞到米香

從妳的爐頂飄來

當妳戴著一串長項鍊

我住進那寶石內

當妳拍攝照片

我出現很多鏡頭

妳不能忘記我！

我始終與妳同在

在妳開會、駕車或甚至

在妳睡眠中！

妳不能忘記我！

看吧，我就在妳身旁
正當月亮對妳說悄悄話

看吧，我就在妳的毛巾裡
正當妳在淋浴時

看吧，我就在妳的光碟裡
在長途車旅中與妳共賞音樂

妳從那天起就引誘我
當我們第一次見面
在太陽陰影下
沒有其他人
僅僅妳和我！

等待彼此見面

等了千年，

可能還不止！

隨同水聲音樂

隨同空氣波浪

隨同鳥的魔術

喔不！單純像小學生上下課

喔不！單純像睡覺做夢

喔不！單純像雨打到妳臉上！

我們等了千年又千年

彼此見面住在此永恆銀河系！

永久 酩農場

Waiting for You for Thousand Years

I am eagerly waiting for you

I am trying to find you from dawn to dark

Left right centre everywhere

In a flower, in a stone, or in volatile atmosphere

Everywhere!

Where are you!

Are you a mermaid in the water?

Are you a fairy in the garden?

Are you belonging to air and water both?

Why could I not be avocado sandwich!

Why could I not be human blanket!

Why could I not be hot tea!

When you cook all night

I can get the smell of your rice

from the top of your oven

When you wear a long necklace

I live in its stones

When you take a picture

I am very much in the lens

You can't forget me!

I will always be with you

In your meeting, driving or even

in your sleep!

You can't forget me!

Just see, I am beside you

While moon whispers in your ear

Just see, I am in your towel

While you are taking shower

Just see, I am in your compact disk

Listening to music with you in a long drive

You are alluring to me from that day

When we met for the first time

In the shadow of the sun

Where no one was

only you and I!

Waiting to meet each other

For thousands of years,

may be more !

With the music of water

With the wave of air

With the magic of a bird

Oh no! it is just like a pupil on and off

Oh no! it is just like sleeping with a dream

Oh no! it is just like a fluke of rain on your face!

We are waiting for thousands and thousands years

To meet each other living in this eternal galaxy!

自殺

此刻我是瘋狂錯亂的小孩

自動自發且透明不會

標示我的夢想實現

夢想欺人張開了

無可比擬的手

不屈地調諧自殺

藝術無盡喜樂專注於

地獄翻轉的特性

心靈每一氣孔

起碼的健康聲響煩人

噴泉逐漸嚮往歇息

Suicide

I am a demented and distracted child of this time

Spontaneity and transparency do not

mark the fruition of my dream

Dream deception has spread out

Its incomparable hand

Untiring harmony of suicide

Ceaseless rapture of artistic endeavour

Infernal somersaults characterize

Every pore of soul

Minimum soundness of health is plagued

Gradually the fountain longed for is losing

自願流亡

我渴望並排坐到天長地久

妳和我一起去旅行

帶著夢中行李

漫步時感覺像碰到妳的手

妳說「不要碰我的手」

眯著眼睛

一瞥妳細緻的嘴唇

妳說「把頭轉過去」

那麼多日子軋了一年或更久

詩對我成為禁制

或者說我已導致生命被詩排斥

我照常吃、散步和對妳說話
確實告訴我真的在流亡中
或者全然沉迷於詩國領域——

可能我難得寫下一行詩
整整這些日子裡
可是我滯留在詩國居所內
我的地址依然相同
——立定在莫測高深的詩海
我的地址依然相同如一
深入莫測高深的詩海

永久酪農場

那裡風動的門還是敞開
那裡幸福從翠葉滴落下來
那裡水鳥從雲而降

我在那裡生活
居住深度比夢還更深
在那裡可能與我心靈交往
我在那裡生活
我會留在那裡直到天長地久
讓生命成為流亡詩國外的生命。

Self-willed Exile

I longed to sit side by side till eternity

You and I were travelling together

With the luggage of a dream

Wandering along I felt like touching your hand

You said "you will not touch me"

With mesmerized eyes

I glanced at your exquisite lips

You said "turn aside your look"

So many days rolled into a year or more

Poetry has been forbidden for me

Or I have led a life ostracized from poetry

I am taking food, walking along and talking to you

Tell me correctly am I really in exile

Or totally steeped in the realm of poesy-

May be I have scarcely written a line of verse

All these days

But I dwell in the abode of poesy

My address is still the same

- Stand of unfathomable ocean of poetry

My address is still the same one

deep in the unfathomable ocean of poetry

Where windy doors remain open

Where bliss trickles down from green leaves

Where water birds descend from clouds

I live there

And dwell in depths deeper than a dream

Where it is possible to be in communion with my soul

I live there

I shall remain there till eternity

Let that life be a life of exile from poetry.

永久 酪農場

簡便包裝的生命

妳整天繞著我旋轉
鳴響在
我生存的核心

月光從
妳被露水濕透的
眼睛滴落在妳
被風遮覆的女體

今夜相當慌張的
是螢火蟲
妳是在那光的
閃閃爍爍中

或是把肉身存在

寫到黑暗裡？

夜靜立

水亦如是

我吸入妳的香味

來自大地

簡便包裝的生命。

遠離星落時

睡眠

乘著我的孤單

我把光剁成碎片

分散在
美人杯裡

多麼燦亮！
多麼無止的靜寂！
多麼無趣的終結！

所有天然色彩
歸一
拼入妳的形體內
或內心深處

妳站出來

在我個人的

存在內

吸收

萬物進入

妳身體曲線裡。

蟋蟀唧唧吱吱

妳碰我

短暫打打鬧鬧

但願我也能碰妳。

在我生命的

破舊帳篷內

一時發熱
妳迅即熄滅
留下
輕輕碰觸的
記憶。

風低聲說
「嗨，詩人怎麼啦
你沉沉睡著
讓你心上人痴等
陪伴夜空。」

用溫柔

滴在眼瞼上

風呢喃，「一對

迷人的眼瞳

向你送秋波。」

心的豎琴奏出

「詩人，為何你在此

卻心不在焉

遠到丘陵

山脈。」

回頭

我啟航前往遙遠地平線

把我的心思捲成球

A Life Wrapped in Ease

Whirling around me all day you

Resound in

The core of my being

Moonlight tickles

From your dew-drenched

Eyes on your wind-

Wrapped *achal*.

Quite restless tonight

Are the fire-flies

Are you in those flickers

Of lights

Or have you written off your corporeal

Existence into darkness?

Night stands still

So does the water

I inhale your scent

From the earth a

Life wrapped in ease.

Far away the stars fall

Asleep

Riding on my loneliness

I chop the light into slices

Distribute them in

A glass of beauty

What luminosity!

What a ceaseless silence!

What a disinterested ending!

All the colours of the nature

Becoming one

Merges into your

Figure or deep down inside

You stand out

In my personal

Existence

Absorbing

Everything into the

Curves of your body.

Crickets sing

You touch me

In ephemeral chipping

I wish I could touch you.

Glowing once

In the worn-out canvas

Of my life

you fizzle out

leaving

memories of gentle

touch.

Whispers the wind

'hi poet how come

You fall asleep while

Your beloved waits

Leaning against the night sky'.

永久 酪農場

With a gentle

Tickle on the eye-lid

The wind murmurs, 'a pair of

Enchanting pupils

Make eye at you'.

The heart's harp plays on

'poet, why you are here when

Your mind wonders off

To far off hills and

Mountains'.

Taken a back

I set sail for a distant horizon

Rolling up my mind into a ball

鄉愁

我聽到鏈條鈴鈴聲
在不息叮噹中持續失落自己
老菸強烈辛辣味使我頭暈
陶醉再度觸動我心靈。

我聽到鏈條鈴鈴聲
感到透過心與靈無法分辨
我謙卑不亞於眾人
我渴望超越黑暗
卻又迷失於無意識深淵裡

我聽到鏈條鈴鈴聲
我從喧嘩當中尋尋覓覓
振作精神面對

卻以更大力量打擊我

感到噓氣透徹椎骨

我聽到鏈條鈴鈴聲

看到自己反映在眾臉上

覆蓋血腥棺木

在泥土掩埋的礫石中

我恐懼顫抖而崩潰

這時隱退的

話語靠近我如一付手銬

扣住我雙手

鏈條嘩啦嘩啦漸去漸杳。

我聽到鏈條鈴鈴聲!!

永久 酪農場

Nostalgia

I hear the jingle of chains

and lose myself continuously in the never ending clinking

Intense pungency of old tobacco makes me dizzy

Again euphoria touches my soul.

I hear the jingle of chains

and feel invisible through my heart and soul

I humble myself like many

I crave to rise above the darkness

But again lose myself into a deep unconsciousness

I hear the jingle of chains

I look for them amidst the clattering

Brace myself to face them

they hit me with larger vigour

feel the breath through the backbone

I hear the jingle of chains

I see myself reflected in the faces

covered with bloody coffin

In the pebbles hidden by earth

and I tremble with fear

And collapse while retreating

words approached me as a shackle

And fasten my two hands

clattering of the chain goes and goes into a gradual wane.

I hear the jingle of chains!!

語言文學類　PG1612　名流詩叢22

永久酪農場

原　　著/阿米紐・拉赫曼（Aminur Rahman）
譯　　者/李魁賢
責任編輯/林世玲
圖文排版/周妤靜
封面設計/蔡瑋筠

發 行 人/宋政坤
法律顧問/毛國樑　律師
出版發行/秀威資訊科技股份有限公司
　　　　114台北市內湖區瑞光路76巷65號1樓
　　　　電話：+886-2-2796-3638　傳真：+886-2-2796-1377
　　　　http://www.showwe.com.tw
劃撥帳號/19563868　戶名：秀威資訊科技股份有限公司
　　　　讀者服務信箱：service@showwe.com.tw
展售門市/國家書店（松江門市）
　　　　104台北市中山區松江路209號1樓
　　　　電話：+886-2-2518-0207　傳真：+886-2-2518-0778
網路訂購/秀威網路書店：http://www.bodbooks.com.tw
　　　　國家網路書店：http://www.govbooks.com.tw

2016年9月　BOD一版
定價：190元
版權所有　翻印必究
本書如有缺頁、破損或裝訂錯誤，請寄回更換

國家圖書館出版品預行編目

永久酪農場 / 阿米紐.拉赫曼(Aminur Rahman) ; 李魁賢譯. -- 一
版. -- 臺北市 : 秀威資訊科技, 2016.09
　　面 ;　　公分. -- (語言文學類 ; PG1612)(名流詩叢 ; 22)
BOD版
譯自 : Perpetual dairy
ISBN 978-986-326-393-7(平裝)

869.3351　　　　　　　　　　　　　　105014175

讀者回函卡

感謝您購買本書，為提升服務品質，請填妥以下資料，將讀者回函卡直接寄回或傳真本公司，收到您的寶貴意見後，我們會收藏記錄及檢討，謝謝！如您需要了解本公司最新出版書目、購書優惠或企劃活動，歡迎您上網查詢或下載相關資料：http:// www.showwe.com.tw

您購買的書名：＿＿＿＿＿＿＿＿＿＿＿＿＿＿＿＿＿＿＿＿＿＿＿＿

出生日期：＿＿＿＿＿年＿＿＿＿＿月＿＿＿＿＿日

學歷：□高中 (含) 以下　　□大專　　□研究所 (含) 以上

職業：□製造業　□金融業　□資訊業　□軍警　□傳播業　□自由業

　　　□服務業　□公務員　□教職　　□學生　□家管　　□其它＿＿＿＿

購書地點：□網路書店　□實體書店　□書展　□郵購　□贈閱　□其他

您從何得知本書的消息？

　　□網路書店　□實體書店　□網路搜尋　□電子報　□書訊　□雜誌

　　□傳播媒體　□親友推薦　□網站推薦　□部落格　□其他＿＿＿＿＿＿

您對本書的評價：(請填代號　1.非常滿意　2.滿意　3.尚可　4.再改進)

　　封面設計＿＿＿　版面編排＿＿＿　內容＿＿＿　文／譯筆＿＿＿　價格＿＿＿

讀完書後您覺得：

　　□很有收穫　□有收穫　□收穫不多　□沒收穫

對我們的建議：＿＿＿＿＿＿＿＿＿＿＿＿＿＿＿＿＿＿＿＿＿＿＿＿

＿＿＿＿＿＿＿＿＿＿＿＿＿＿＿＿＿＿＿＿＿＿＿＿＿＿＿＿＿＿＿＿＿＿

＿＿＿＿＿＿＿＿＿＿＿＿＿＿＿＿＿＿＿＿＿＿＿＿＿＿＿＿＿＿＿＿＿＿

＿＿＿＿＿＿＿＿＿＿＿＿＿＿＿＿＿＿＿＿＿＿＿＿＿＿＿＿＿＿＿＿＿＿

11466
台北市內湖區瑞光路 76 巷 65 號 1 樓
秀威資訊科技股份有限公司　　　收
BOD 數位出版事業部

....

（請沿線對折寄回，謝謝！）

姓　　名：＿＿＿＿＿＿＿＿＿　年齡：＿＿＿＿　性別：□女　□男

郵遞區號：□□□□□

地　　址：＿＿＿＿＿＿＿＿＿＿＿＿＿＿＿＿＿＿＿＿＿

聯絡電話：(日)＿＿＿＿＿＿＿＿＿　(夜)＿＿＿＿＿＿＿＿＿

E-mail：＿＿＿＿＿＿＿＿＿＿＿＿＿＿＿＿＿＿＿＿＿